GAIL HAS TO DO *SOMETHING*!

Gail took a sheet of paper out of her notebook. This is what she wrote:

> Dear Matthew,
> I am very, very sorry.
> > Your friend,
> > Gail

When she got up to sharpen her pencil, she dropped the note on his desk. Back in her seat, she watched the back of his head, but he never turned around. Just as they were packing up their books to go home, Matthew dropped a note on her desk. This is what he had written:

> Gail:
> Just leave me alone.
> > Your former friend,
> > Matthew

Your Former Friend, Matthew

by LouAnn Gaeddert

illustrated by Mary Beth Schwark

A BANTAM SKYLARK BOOK®
TORONTO · NEW YORK · LONDON · SYDNEY · AUCKLAND

For my nephew, Nate Meldrim

*This low-priced Bantam Book
was printed from new plates. It
contains the complete text of
the original hard-cover edition.*
NOT ONE WORD HAS BEEN OMITTED.

RL 4, 008–011

YOUR FORMER FRIEND, MATTHEW
*A Bantam Book / published by arrangement with
E. P. Dutton, Inc.*

PRINTING HISTORY
*E. P. Dutton edition published May 1984
A Selection of Weekly Reader Children's Book Clubs
(Xerox Education Publications)
Bantam Skylark edition / October 1985*

ISBN 0-553-15345-5

Published simultaneously in the United States and Canada

---

*Bantam Books are published by Bantam Books, Inc. Its trademark,
consisting of the words "Bantam Books" and the portrayal of a rooster,
is Registered in U.S. Patent and Trademark Office and in other
countries. Marca Registrada. Bantam Books, Inc., 666 Fifth Avenue,
New York, New York 10103.*

PRINTED IN THE UNITED STATES OF AMERICA

CW   0 9 8 7 6 5 4 3 2

C·H·A·P·T·E·R

1

The best day of school is the last day of school. At noon, Gail Walden and Matthew Morrison ran out of the school yard together, shouting good-byes to their friends. They jumped off the curb and ran across the street. They ran until they had to stop for a red light. Then they grabbed a signpost and swung around and around until the light turned green.

They ran until they were in the lobby of their apartment building. There they threw themselves on a big, lumpy sofa and lay gasping for breath. Matthew's blond hair was streaked brown with sweat. Gail's glasses were sliding off her nose. Her light brown hair hung limply around her face. That morning it had been pulled into a neat ponytail. Gail's hair didn't stay neat. She didn't care.

"Oh, what a beautiful mornin'," she sang at the top of her voice.

"Oh, what a beautiful day," Matthew joined in. "I've got . . ."

They stopped as Amanda Eliott walked quietly through the lobby door. She was in their class, and she lived in their building, too. Amanda was pretty, neat, quiet—"a perfect little lady," adults said approvingly. No one ever called Gail a perfect little lady.

"Hi, Lady Amanda," Matthew said, raising his hand to wave at her. "I'm off for a whole summer in the country. Gail is going to a girlee campee. . . ."

Gail kicked him. "Camp's a month. Then we're going to my grandmother's in Vermont. Then two weeks on Cape Cod with my cousin."

"My father is taking me abroad," said Amanda. "He has to go to Paris on business, and then we're going to Switzerland, maybe to Italy."

"Really?" Gail and Matthew said together as they sat up on the old sofa to get a good look at Amanda.

"Yes, really. I have lots of folders and things about places we're going. Maybe you'd like to see . . ."

"No," Gail said quickly. "I mean, we'd like to see them but we can't. Not now, anyway. . . ."

"That's OK. See you in the fall." Amanda stepped into the open elevator, and the door closed behind her.

That was one good thing about Amanda. She knew when she wasn't wanted. Gail sometimes wished Amanda were nastier. Then Gail wouldn't feel guilty about not wanting to include her on a special day like this. This was the last time she would see Matthew for ten whole weeks. He was her best friend. She didn't want to share him.

"Glad you said that, pal." Matthew gave Gail a little sock on her shoulder. "I've got this great idea about rocks."

"What about rocks?"

"I think we should collect rocks for our science fair project next fall. Maybe we could get some books on rocks at the library today. During the summer we can each collect rocks. Then next fall, when everyone is trying to think up science fair projects, we'll be all set. What do you think?"

Matthew always had good ideas. They'd been friends since they were babies. Their parents were friends, too. On days when Matthew's mother didn't get home from work before Matthew got home from school, he came to her apartment. They spent most afternoons together anyway.

Often they had the same thoughts at the same time. Like now. They jumped up from the sofa together and headed for the stairs. Gail went to her apartment on the second floor. Matthew ran on to his apartment on the fourth floor. He didn't have to tell Gail where he was going or what he was going to do. She knew.

A few minutes later, he was back at her apartment. Both of them were dressed in their after-school uniforms—cut-off jeans, polo shirts and sneakers with holes in the tops.

"Can you believe it?" Gail asked, sticking a finger through the hole in the top of her sneakers. "My mother won't let me take these good old sneakers to camp."

Matthew nodded his sympathy. "My mother said she is going to throw my old friends down the incinerator this afternoon before we leave. Good-bye, old friends," he said, patting his sneakers. "Good-bye, Gail's old friends," he said, patting her toes.

Benji, Gail's little brother, laughed. "I have brand-new sneakers. See?" He lifted his foot up to Matthew. "Boy, can I run fast in them. Want to see how fast I can run?"

"No," said Matthew, turning back to Gail and pulling money out of his pocket. "My mother left this with a note: *For celebration ice-cream cones.*"

When Gail's mother called them to lunch, Gail told her about the cones.

"Can I go too?" asked Benji.

"No you can't," Gail growled.

Mother gave Gail one of her why-can't-you-be-nice-to-Benji? looks.

"You're sure lucky to be an only child," Gail told Matthew as they walked to the ice-cream store.

They studied the list of flavors for a long time. At last Matthew chose bubble gum flavor and gave Gail the first bite.

"Yuck," she said, holding her cone out for Matthew. It was her all-time favorite, peppermint stick with chocolate sprinkles.

"At least mine is different. I'm adventurous. You always have peppermint stick with chocolate sprinkles."

When they got to the library, they wiped their sticky hands on their cut-off jeans and went upstairs to the children's room. The librarian showed them the shelf with rock books.

"Remember," she said, "if you're going away for the summer, you can check out ten books and return them in September."

There weren't many rock books, and some of them were like picture books for babies. They chose the four fattest books, and then Matthew went off to look for science fiction books and Gail went to look for mysteries.

Sure enough, Matthew had three science fiction books to check out. But he also had a biography of someone named Jackie Robinson, a book on body building, and one called *How To Star at Basketball.*

"Good grief, Matthew," Gail exclaimed. "What do you want to read those books for?"

"Because."

"Because why?"

"Just because." Matthew glared at her.

Walking home, Gail thought about the strange books in Matthew's pile.

"Are you thinking about becoming a muscleman this summer?"

Matthew didn't answer.

"Come on, Matthew. Tell me. We don't have secrets."

"You wouldn't understand."

"Why wouldn't I understand?" Gail felt herself getting mad.

"Because you're a girl."

When they got to the lobby, Matthew nodded over his stack of books to Gail's sneakers. "Good-bye, old friends," he said.

"Have a good time this summer, Matthew." Gail felt a strange lump in her throat.

"Enjoy the girlees at your campee." Matthew looked straight at her and grinned.

Gail couldn't sock him because her arms were full of books, so she glared.

"Good-bye, old pal," he said softly. "See you in the fall. Don't forget to collect lots of rocks."

"Good-bye, Matthew."

Gail went upstairs to her apartment thinking about Matthew. What a friend!

C·H·A·P·T·E·R

2

Gail began collecting rocks during her first hour at camp. By the end of the month, she had filled two big boxes. The camp director asked her to exhibit her collection in the dining hall.

"We should have rented a truck," her dad grumbled when the family picked her up at the end of the camp session. There wasn't enough room in the trunk of their car for both boxes and her camping gear. Gail had to ride all the way to Vermont with her feet on top of a box.

Rock hunting in Vermont was even better than it had been at camp. Everywhere she went, there were white marble chunks. Her grandmother took her to a rock shop and bought her a geode with amethyst crystals in the center, a small piece of jade, and an uncut garnet. Gail also had time to study her books and to begin to identify some of her specimens. She was loading her new rocks in another box when her father put his foot down.

"There simply isn't room for three big boxes of

rocks. Either you get rid of one box or we'll tie *you* on the top of the car." He helped her decide which rocks to discard.

After Vermont, they went to Cape Cod. Her parents and Benji spent two nights and then drove back to the city, taking the rocks with them.

Gail's cousin, Linda Lou, had the world's largest collection of Barbie dolls. Even on nice days, she would rather sit on the porch with her dolls than go to the beach. Gail hated dolls. She always had.

So Gail left Linda Lou on the porch, dressing Barbie for dates with Ken, while she went to the beach by herself. She picked up beautiful rocks smoothed by the waves, and a few perfect shells.

One night after dinner, her uncle asked to see her beach collection. Linda Lou dressed Barbie for bed while Linda Lou's father examined each rock and helped Gail identify some of them. Then he took an Indian arrowhead out of his pocket.

"My grandfather, your great grandfather, found this when he was a boy. I want you to have it."

"Wait till my friend Matthew sees this," Gail exclaimed, throwing her arms around her uncle. "I started collecting rocks because Matthew asked me to. Now I think I'm going to study rocks for the rest of my life."

"You want to be a geologist?"

"Do you think I could?"

"I'm going to be a model when I grow up," said Linda Lou.

Before Gail boarded the bus that would take her back to New York, the bus driver lifted her duffel bag to stash it with the other luggage in the bottom of the bus. "You got rocks in there?" he joked.

"As a matter of fact, I have," said Gail. "Forty-seven, to be exact."

Her parents and Benji were waiting for her as she got off the bus in New York. Her dad lifted the duffel bag and groaned.

"Not more rocks," he grumbled.

She opened the bag and pulled out two plastic bags of rocks. "I'll carry them," she said. "Just wait until Matthew sees them! Are they home yet?"

"His parents are home, but Matthew is staying in the country with a friend. He's coming home the day before school starts," said Mother.

"What friend?"

"A boy he pals around with in the country. I don't know his name. I think he lives down the road from their house. Come on. Let's hurry home. We have a surprise for you."

Gail tried to find out more about the surprise. "How big is it?"

"Big," said Benji.

"As big as my duffel bag?"

"Bigger."

"As big as Dad?"

"Bigger."

"As big as Grandma's house?"

"Smaller."

"Is it alive?"

"No."

"Will I like it?"

"I don't know," said Mother, "but you need it."

Gail quit asking questions. How could something she needed be a surprise? She needed a new jacket, school shoes and a new notebook. Surprises should be fun.

"It's in your room," Dad said as he unlocked the door to their apartment.

She ran down the hall, threw open her door and gasped. Her room had been painted a lovely soft shade of yellow. Yellow was her favorite color. Her bed was still there, but all her old furniture was gone. Instead, she now had a big desk with cabinets on either side. Above were shelves that went all the way to the ceiling and a ladder so that she could reach them.

"Oh!" She hugged her father. "Oh!" She hugged her mother. She even hugged Benji. "Thank you, thank you, thank you," she squealed. "Wait until Matthew sees this!"

She searched in her plastic bags until she found the arrowhead. She showed it to her family, and then she placed it right in the center of one of the lower shelves.

In the week before school started, Gail was busy getting her room in order. She and her mother bought a new bedspread and a blotter for her desk. She arranged all of her books in alphabetical order, just like a library. She arranged her rocks just like a museum. She even labeled some of them.

Sunday afternoon she went to see if Matthew was home. She couldn't wait to show him her collection.

"His train doesn't get in until nine," Mrs. Morrison said.

"Why is he coming so late?" Gail asked.

"He wanted to stay in the country as long as possible. He's had a wonderful summer, Gail."

"What's he been doing?"

"Swimming every day. Playing basketball. Camping out."

"Who with?"

"Boys he knows up there."

"Tell him I have surprises for him. Tell him I'll see him in the morning." Gail didn't like to hear about Matthew's having good times without her. She ran back to her own apartment.

The next morning, as soon as she was ready for school, she ran up to Matthew's apartment. He usually stopped by for her, but she had so many things to tell him that she couldn't wait.

She rang his doorbell with her usual three short rings. Silence. No footsteps on the other side of the door. No nothing. She rang again. She rang a third time. His parents would have left for work. Where was he?

He couldn't have gone to school without her. Maybe he was sick, lying there alone on the floor, gasping for breath. On the other hand, maybe he had taken the elevator down to her apartment while she was running up the stairs to his apartment. They never used the elevator, but maybe he was tired this morning after his busy summer.

Gail ran back to her apartment. Matthew hadn't been there. She ran on down to the lobby and out to the street and on to school. Matthew must be sick. If he were not in the school yard, she'd have to come back to rescue him.

When Gail turned the corner, she saw Amanda ahead. From half a block away, Gail could see that Amanda was dressed in all new clothes, a pastel plaid dress with a ruffle around the bottom, white knee socks without a wrinkle, and pink shoes. Her black hair shone in the sunlight, and the sides were held back with a pink bow.

Gail walked along behind Amanda until they were almost at the school. Then she called and ran to catch up with her. She could feel Amanda looking her over. It was hot, so Gail was wearing her coolest dress, blue seersucker with no collar, no sleeves and no trim. She wore red sneakers with no socks. Suddenly Gail felt plain.

"Have a nice summer, Mandy?" Gail knew that Amanda hated to be called Mandy.

"Divine," Amanda cooed. "In Paris, I had a French companion who took me all over the city. We spoke nothing but French. . . ."

Other girls from their class were soon clustered

around Amanda, listening with envy to every word about her divine summer. Gail walked away.

She had to find Matthew. She did. He was shooting baskets with other boys. A moment of disappointment, because he didn't need rescuing, melted into joy. It was good to see old Matthew again!

"Hey, Matthew," Gail shouted as she ran toward him.

He looked up, waved and went right back to his game, dribbling the ball away from a much bigger boy and throwing it from half a court away directly into the basket.

"What a shot," a boy named Jay shouted.

Even Gail was surprised. Matthew had learned a lot from that book he had checked out of the library.

The school bell rang. The boys left their game to line up in the yard. Gail waited for Matthew.

"I rang your bell," she said. "Why didn't you come by for me? Did you have a nice summer?"

"Sorry about that." Matthew grinned sheepishly. "Yeah, I had a great summer. How about you?"

Gail started to tell him about her creepy cousin and then about her rocks, but before she could get started, Matthew had walked on ahead of her to join Jay and some other boys from their class.

"Did you collect rocks?" she called after him. "I have some wonderful specimens to show you. After school . . ."

Matthew didn't even hear her. Gail stood alone for a minute. What had happened to Matthew?

C·H·A·P·T·E·R 3

The first morning of the school year is always the same, Gail thought. The teacher introduced herself. Her name was Mrs. Johnson. There was nothing special about her appearance, and she began in the usual way, asking each student to introduce himself and tell something about his summer.

Amanda, of course, talked about her summer on "the continent." At least she had something different to say. Lots of kids had been to camp or to visit their grandmothers or to the beach. Gail couldn't even talk about the rocks she had collected, because that was a surprise for the science fair.

Matthew's talk made Gail mad. He and three other boys had biked twenty miles and then climbed a ridge to a campsite. They had spent the night and cooked all their own food over a campfire and then biked home.

The teacher asked the question Gail wanted to ask: "There were no adults with you? Just four boys all about your age?"

Matthew grinned. "We had a dog chaperone. Actually the campsite belongs to the uncle of one of the guys. We took his dog with us. My friend's uncle told my parents that if we got in trouble, his dog would come for help. But we didn't need any help, and the dog just slept up there with us."

How could Matthew have so much fun without her? Who were these boys who were his pals? Why hadn't she heard all of this first? Matthew's hair was still blond. His mouth was still wide, and he still grinned a lot. Still, he seemed to be a stranger. He didn't even look at Gail while he talked.

She was mad at Matthew all morning. Then at lunchtime, she saw him waiting at the end of the table assigned to their class. Of course he was waiting for her. They'd eaten lunch together every school day since first grade. She pushed toward him eagerly.

But when she got to the table, Matthew was already seated—between two boys and across from three more boys. As she watched, he turned to Jay. She couldn't hear what he was saying, but she could tell from his gestures that he was talking about basketball.

Sitting with the girls at the other end of the table, Gail thought about Jay. What was so interesting about him? He'd entered their class in the middle of the past year. He was the tallest boy in the class, and he always seemed to have a ball in his hand or under his arm.

Matthew's laugh rose over the other voices in the lunchroom. Gail couldn't stand it. She turned to Joyce, sitting on her left. Joyce was weird. Matthew called her the Mad Scientist. Anything you wanted to know about how far it is to Mars or the life cycle of a worm, Joyce could tell you. The really strange thing about her was that she kept her face hidden behind her hair. She had beautiful, reddish blonde hair which she wore carefully combed over her face. She'd worn it that way for so long that Gail couldn't remember what her face looked like. Some of the kids said she had a purple birthmark on her cheek. Others said that her nose was huge.

"How was your summer, Joyce?" Gail asked.

Joyce shrugged her shoulders. "So-so."

Who wanted to talk to a curtain of hair? Gail turned to her right. Amanda was still on the subject of Europe. Parts of Switzerland looked just like you'd expect if you'd read *Heidi*. The Sistine Chapel didn't look like a church at all. The tourists stood shoulder to shoulder and looked up at Michelangelo's famous paintings on the ceiling through opera glasses. The shops in Paris were *très* chic.

Gail wished Matthew could have heard Amanda using French phrases. It was revolting. She tried to tell the girls about Linda Lou and the Barbie dolls, but no one would listen.

Gail walked home from school with Amanda and another girl who lived near them.

"Tell us about your summer, Gail," Amanda said. "Did you like camp? How was the Cape?"

At last Gail had a chance to tell about her boring cousin, but her story sounded dull, even to her. She cut it short.

When they got to the lobby, Amanda said that she was meeting some of the girls in the park. She invited Gail to come along. "I'll stop by for you."

"Don't," Gail said gruffly. "I might come later. I have things to do."

In their apartment, Benji was giving their mother a minute-by-minute account of his whole first day in second grade. When he stopped to gulp down his juice, Mother asked about her day.

"Nothing special." Gail went to her room to change into cut-off jeans and a polo shirt.

She lay down on her bed and looked up at her rock exhibit. She'd been so proud of it, and now Matthew wouldn't even come to look at it. She felt tears behind her eyes. Gail was not a cryer, so she sat up and thumped her fist into her pillow until she felt better. Then she put her best agate in her pocket, told her mother she was going to the park, and left the apartment.

Their park was not a park at all. It was mostly cement. It was in the block across the street from their apartment house. Matthew always called it their home away from home, because they had spent so much time there.

Without Matthew, the park seemed strange. Gail

walked through the gate nearest her corner. Just inside the gate, old men sat under a tree playing checkers and chess.

"Hello there, girl," one of the old men called to her. "When I saw your sidekick go through here without you, I wondered if you'd moved away. I'm glad you're still here. Hope you had a nice summer."

"Thanks, Mr. Stein. I'm glad to see you too."

She walked on slowly kicking a pebble in front of her. She kicked it past the benches, where young mothers sat with their babies and tiny children. She kicked it toward the baseball diamond, where Matthew was standing waiting for his turn at bat. She walked toward him, but he didn't seem to see her. She went on without speaking.

"Hey, Gail, down here," one of the girls called from the lower level, where hopscotch squares had been painted on the cement. Amanda was there. She gave Gail a piece of candy from Italy. Roseanne was there with her baby brother in a stroller. There were so many children in Roseanne's family that she always had to take care of at least one of them after school. Lillian and Dora were there together as always. They'd been best friends as long as she and Matthew had been best friends. They even dressed alike some of the time. Matthew called them the Bobbsey Twins.

Gail played hopscotch the rest of the afternoon. When it was beginning to be going-home time, Gail kept one eye on the baseball diamond.

"It's time for me to be getting home," Gail said as soon as Matthew's game seemed to be breaking up.

"But we're not through," Dora wailed.

"Sorry," Gail said in her most positive voice. She dropped her marker. "I have to go right now."

She walked off quickly in the direction of the gate nearest home. Matthew was walking toward that gate too. The other boys were leaving by another gate. Gail timed her steps carefully. Just as Matthew was about to go through the gate, she took the agate out of her pocket and ran as fast as she could. She dashed through the gate, bumping right into Matthew. She didn't knock him down, but she hit him hard enough that he could not ignore her. She also dropped her agate.

"Oh. Sorry, Matthew. I didn't see you. Now where is my agate?"

Gail got down on her hands and knees and started looking for it. For a minute, she was afraid she had lost it, but it had just rolled farther than she had planned. She handed the rock to Matthew who was grinning down at her.

"How do you like it? I found it at the shore. I picked up boxes and boxes of rocks. Want to see them?"

Matthew stood turning the agate over in his hand. "I don't know. I have a lot . . ."

"Please, Matthew. Please come down after dinner. I want you to see my new room and my rocks. I want . . ." She stopped. She wasn't about to tell

21

Matthew that what she really wanted was to be his old buddy.

Gail was just finishing dinner when she heard the three short taps of the doorbell.

"It's Matthew," Benji shouted as he ran to the door.

"Hi, Benji," Gail heard Matthew greet her little brother. "Who do you think's going to win the pennant?"

"Philadelphia," said Benji.

"We'll see." Matthew sounded as if he knew something nobody else knew about the pennant race.

Gail didn't even know who was playing. She watched with amazement as the two boys approached the table. Last year Matthew had agreed with her that Benji was a first-class pain. Now he was talking baseball to the little kid, almost as if they were equals. Benji was staring up at him with adoration.

Gail's parents greeted Matthew warmly. They asked about his summer and told him how glad they were to see him. Couldn't they see that this kid standing in front of them was not the same Matthew they thought they knew? He was a stranger.

"Come see my rocks." Gail got up from the table.

"Can I . . . ?" Benji started timidly.

"No," said Gail.

"He just wants to look," said Matthew.

So they went off to her room, Gail and Matthew and Benji. Benji was never allowed beyond the door to Gail's room. To give him credit, he wasn't a nuisance. In fact, he didn't say anything. He didn't even touch anything. Matthew exclaimed over her new furniture and then climbed the ladder to examine her rock collection.

Mother called Benji to go to bed. A little later, Matthew announced that he had to go home.

"Tomorrow night I'll come look at your rocks," Gail said.

"What rocks?" Matthew looked truly surprised.

"The rocks you said you were going to collect for our science fair project."

"The rocks I said . . ." Matthew hit the side of his head with the palm of his hand. "I forgot all about that. I did start to read one of the books, but then I just got so busy I forgot all about rocks. The only rocks I have are in my head. Oh well, you've got a good start on your science fair project. Maybe Jay and I can do something together."

Gail stared at him. She had spent the whole summer working on a project that had been his idea, and he had forgotten all about it. She walked with him to the front door.

"You're not coming by for me in the morning either, are you?"

"No. I'm meeting Jay early so we can shoot baskets for a half hour before school starts. 'Bye, Gail. Thanks for showing me your rocks." Matthew didn't punch her in the shoulder. He didn't call her old pal.

C · H · A · P · T · E ·

4

The second day of school was just as bad as the first day had been. After school, the girls made plans to meet at the park again. Gail didn't go. She didn't want to play with them. She didn't want to hear more about Amanda's summer. She didn't want to do anything.

She didn't even want her snack. She went to her room, lay down on her bed, and tried to sleep. Her mother came in and sat on the bed beside her. She stroked Gail's hair.

"I know you miss Matthew," she said softly.

"I don't miss Matthew. I don't even like him. I hate him." Gail was screaming.

"No you don't. You and Matthew have been good friends for too long. You're hurt. I was afraid this would happen one day. I had hoped that you would both find other friends at the same time. Matthew has found new friends. You've got to find a new friend, too."

Mother was great for substitutes. When cat died, Mother suggested that they go r get a kitten. Gail hadn't wanted a new had wanted her good old cat. She didn't wan friend now.

"Aren't your summer books due at the library?" Mother asked. "Why don't you return them?"

Gail turned away and faced the wall.

"Look, darling, Matthew will . . ."

Gail didn't want to talk about Matthew. She got up and began shoving her library books into a shopping bag.

It was such a nice day outside that no one Gail knew was at the library except Joyce. She was peering through strands of hair at the fiction titles. Gail couldn't imagine Joyce reading a story. To know so much, she had to spend all her time reading the encyclopedia.

"Hi, Joyce. What kinds of books you looking for?"

"Hi, Gail. Mysteries. Know any good ones?"

"You like mysteries? They're my favorite." Gail picked out a few that she knew were particularly good and handed them to Joyce. "You read these?"

"No. I just discovered mysteries. I don't like most kids' books, but I like to follow the clues to find out who did it."

Gail selected some books for herself, and she and Joyce went to the check-out counter together.

"Most of the girls are at the park. Why aren't you there?" Gail asked.

"If you want the truth, it's that I'm already tired of hearing about Amanda's summer."

"Me too."

Joyce was like a mystery, but Gail didn't have enough clues to figure her out.

The rest of the week was just like the beginning of the week, boring. School was all right. Mrs. Johnson certainly didn't believe in a slow start. She assigned a book report and said there would be a book report due every two weeks for the rest of the year. She assigned everyone to committees to make reports on Israel for social studies. Gail tried to get herself on the same committee with Matthew. It didn't work.

After school was the miserable time. One afternoon she went to the park. Other afternoons she read in her room.

Saturday morning, Gail woke to the sound of rain beating against her window. She lay in bed feeling glum. All of a sudden, she had a brightening thought: Monopoly. This was the perfect day for an all-day game.

She jumped out of bed and darted to her closet for her jeans. They weren't there. She looked around her room. How could it have become so messy in such a short time? She finally found her jeans under the bed. She knew her mother wouldn't let her do anything until her room was clean, so she carried a week's supply of dirty clothes to the hamper and got the vacuum cleaner. By ten o'clock she'd eaten breakfast and put her room back in order. When Mother came to check the room, she asked Gail if she'd made plans for the day.

"Monopoly," said Gail. "Could I make a plate of sandwiches? I'll ask Matthew and Amanda down. It's more fun with three. We'll play all day." She stopped and thought about Matthew. "Maybe there will be four. Maybe Matthew will want to bring Jay." Gail headed for the kitchen.

"Why don't you invite your friends and then make the sandwiches?" Mother called after her. "In case they have other plans."

"Other plans? What other plans could they have on a day like this?"

"I don't know, but you'd better ask them before you make the sandwiches."

Gail ran up to Matthew's apartment first. Matthew answered her three short rings, but instead of inviting her in, he stood in the doorway. He listened to her talk about the all-day game of Monopoly and lunch and her suggestion that he might like to invite Jay.

"Sorry," he said when she finally came to a stop. "We've made plans for the day."

"On a day like this?" Gail was both surprised and angry. "You can't play ball today. What are you going to do?"

"We're going to the movies."

"Who?"

"Jay and Mike—maybe Peter—and me."

"What are you going to see?"

"*Beyond Mars.*"

"I've heard about that. I've heard it's a great movie. . . ." Gail stopped to give Matthew a chance to invite her to come too.

There was silence. Then the silliest thing happened. Gail felt tears floating behind her eyes. She sniffed and turned and ran to the stairs.

"Hey, Gail," Matthew called after her. "I'm sorry."

"Forget it," Gail shouted back. "I can't stand science fiction movies anyway."

Monopoly isn't much fun with just two, but Gail went up to Amanda's apartment anyway. Maybe they could ask Joyce to come. But Amanda had gone shopping with her grandmother. Her father didn't think they'd be back until late afternoon.

Gail's mother turned off the vacuum cleaner as she came in. "The game all set?"

"No." Gail didn't try to explain. She just ran to her room, slammed the door and flung herself on her bed.

At lunchtime, Mother suggested that maybe she'd like to take Benji to the movies. He wanted to see *Beyond Mars.* Gail didn't want to take him, but she did. Luckily she got in and out of the theater without seeing Matthew.

Soon after she got home, Amanda came down. "My dad said you were up to see me this morning,"

she said. "I'm sorry I was out. Grandma and I had lunch at the Plaza. Want to come up to see my new winter coat? It's blue with a velvet collar."

Instead, Gail invited Amanda to see her new room, and she was glad she did. Amanda's eyes lit up at the sight of the new shelves and the ladder. "Terrific," she exclaimed. She climbed the ladder and picked up the geode. "Beautiful."

Amanda looked at all of Gail's rocks. She asked questions about where they came from. She held them as if she really liked them. She didn't even mention Europe.

Mother came to the door. "Would you like to stay for dinner?" she asked Amanda. "We're having spaghetti."

"Oh thank you!" Amanda sounded as if she were going to say yes. "But I can't. My dad is making a pot roast. He'd be disappointed if I didn't eat it with him. He's really getting to be a very good cook. So am I."

"I'll bet you are." Mother stroked Amanda's hair.

Gail hadn't thought before about who cooked for Amanda since her mother died. At first, of course, Amanda had a baby-sitter. Her grandmother came when her father had to be out of town. Most of the time, Amanda and her father were by themselves. Gail wondered if Amanda still missed her mother.

C·H·A·P·T·E·R
5

The second and third weeks of school were no better than the first, except that Gail no longer expected to be Matthew's buddy. She saw him at school. Sometimes he ignored her and sometimes he said "Hi." She looked out her window and saw him running around the block before breakfast. She saw him in the school yard playing basketball or handball and in the park playing basketball or baseball. He was always grinning. Somehow Matthew's grin made Gail want to stamp her feet and howl.

Gail usually walked to and from school with Amanda. Amanda didn't talk about her European trip so much, but she still used French phrases. When anyone else would say "Golly" or "Gosh," Amanda said "*Tiens.*"

Gail ate lunch with the girls and usually found herself sitting next to Joyce. They spent one whole lunch period discussing books. The next day Joyce brought a pencil and a piece of paper to lunch to write down the names of some mysteries Gail liked.

During the fourth week, she heard about the science fair, from Benji of all people. "Every kid in the school is supposed to make an ex-ex-exhibit," he announced at dinner.

"What kind of an ex-ex-exhibit are you going to make?" Gail mocked.

"A burglar alarm."

"Come again?"

"A burglar alarm. I'm going to make a burglar alarm."

"That's the dumbest thing I ever heard. What's scientific about a burglar alarm?"

"Hush, Gail." Dad spoke in his angry voice. "Personally, I think a burglar alarm is a very good idea. How are you going to make it, son?"

"I have to get a big battery and a bell and a switch kind of thing. I'll tie a string to the switch and to the door so when you open the door the bell will ring. Will you help me, Dad?"

"And what are you going to do with your burglar alarm?" Gail asked. "Are you going to sell it to a bank?"

"I'm going to keep you out of my room."

The next day, Mrs. Johnson told her class about the science fair. She asked if anyone had any ideas.

Joyce's hand shot up. "I've already begun. I'm

breeding guppies. I started with two cheap guppies. The pet store calls them wild guppies. They were small and gray. When they had babies I bred the largest ones with the longest tails with one another. I've kept on breeding the best guppies until now I have some that are very large and have very long tails. I've kept records of how many were born each time and what they looked like. Mine is an experiment in genetics. It's the same idea as breeding corn to get bigger ears or flowers to get different colors."

"What a great idea!" exclaimed Gail. Boy, was that Joyce smart! "It'll be the best exhibit in the whole fair!"

"I think it's a wonderful idea, too," said Mrs. Johnson. "What are you planning, Gail?"

"I'm going to exhibit my rock collection."

"That would be fine for a hobby show, Gail," the teacher said. "But it won't do for the science fair. You'll have to use your rocks as part of an experiment or present them in some way that has meaning scientifically. Think about what geologists do. What are you going to do, Matthew?"

"I don't know." Matthew shook his head as if he were bewildered by the whole idea.

"Maybe Matthew and I will build a catapult," Jay suggested.

"What's scientific about a catapult?" Gail asked.

"It will be a very scientific catapult." Matthew glared at Gail. "We'll explain all the principles of physics involved."

Gail sat next to Joyce at lunch. "I think your project is terrific," she said.

"Have you thought about what you are going to do with your rocks?"

"Maybe I'll do tests to identify them. I read about the tests in a book I checked out of the library this summer. I better check it out again. Do you think that will be scientific enough?"

"Yes." Joyce sounded positive.

"My project has really got to be good."

"I know. You want it to be better than Matthew's project."

Gail nodded. How did Joyce know that? "Would you like to see my rocks? We could meet at the library and then go to my apartment."

Joyce agreed.

The book Gail wanted was on the shelf, and she checked it out again. Joyce looked carefully at each of Gail's rocks, holding her hair up off her forehead so that she could look down at the rocks while her face was still hidden from Gail.

"You'd better go to the Museum of Natural History," Joyce announced.

Gail groaned. When she was little, her parents took her to the Museum of Natural History several times. Once she started school, her class had been taken there every year.

"Have you been to the rock and mineral room?" Joyce asked.

"Didn't know there was one."

"So let's go on Saturday."

"Who'll take us?" Gail asked.

"We'll go by ourselves."

"On the subway? By ourselves? Have you really gone on the subway by yourself?"

"No. But I know the way." Joyce spoke as if taking the subway were like walking to the library.

"Alone? On the subway?" Gail's mother was stunned when she heard the plan that night at dinner.

"There's nothing to it," said Gail in her most matter-of-fact voice. "If we get lost, we can just ask someone."

"That's a good idea," said Dad. "City children have to learn to go alone on the subway. I'll bring you a subway map. You can always telephone if you get lost, and we'll come and rescue you."

"But with Joyce?" Mother looked as if she might be sick. She turned to Dad. "She was here this afternoon. She wears her hair combed down over her face."

"Why is that?" Dad asked.

"I don't know. Some kids say she has a birthmark on her cheek, and others say she has a funny nose. I don't think either of those are true. She had short bangs in first grade, and I don't remember anything strange about her face. I don't know why she's never had her bangs cut since then. But she's smart. Boy is she smart! Maybe she's letting her hair grow as part of a scientific experiment."

"What kind of experiment?" ask Mother.

Gail couldn't answer that.

"How does she see to do her schoolwork and to walk the streets?" Dad asked.

"When she reads, she pushes her hair up over the back of her hand so it's away from her face and she can look down at her books. When she's out on the street, she separates it so that she has a little slot in front of each eye. She has blue eyes."

While they were talking, Benji looked from one member of his family to another. At first he looked puzzled. Then he grinned. "Maybe her hair is like an all-year-round Halloween mask. Or a tent. She can hide under her hair and look out, and nobody knows what's inside."

Benji pushed his own hair forward so that it covered his forehead. It wasn't long enough to cover his eyes.

"You need a haircut," Dad said.

Mother left the table to phone Joyce's mother.

C·H·A·P·T·E·R

6

Saturday morning Gail met Joyce at the subway station. In her jeans pockets, she had two subway tokens, money for lunch and telephone calls, a small notebook and a pencil.

In her head, she had a thousand words of warning from her mother: *Don't talk to strangers. Ask a policeman if you get lost. Don't talk to strangers. Keep your eyes open. Don't talk to strangers. Get on and off trains quickly. Don't . . .*

In her hand, she carried the subway map her dad had brought to her.

Gail and Joyce walked down the steps and put their tokens into the turnstile. They walked toward the sign that said To Manhattan and down another flight of steps. The E train was just clacking its way into the station. It stopped and the doors opened. The girls found two seats together. Gail unfolded her map and showed Joyce the route her father had marked on it.

The train started again and was soon swaying through a long dark tunnel which seemed to have no end. Gail was beginning to feel a little twinge of worry when lights appeared outside the windows and the train slowed to a stop. The sign in the station said Queens Plaza. Gail checked her map. They were right on the route her dad had marked. One after another they passed through the stations marked on the map. Gail stood up at Fifth Avenue.

They got out of the train at Seventh Avenue and changed to another train. At the next stop they changed again. The first sign they saw when they got out at 81st Street was an arrow pointing in the direction of the Museum of Natural History.

Getting around New York by subway was an overrated skill, Gail thought as they walked directly out of the station into the basement of the museum. Benji could have made this trip.

In the past, Gail had been taken to the museum by grown-ups who decided which parts they would visit. Today, studying the plan of the museum with Joyce, Gail realized that there were whole sections she had never seen. Meteorites, Minerals and Gems were in the far corner of the first floor. Fortunately, there were signs to direct them.

At the entrance to the gem and mineral collection, Gail gasped. The dark space ahead was like a huge carpeted cave. It was on many levels and there were little rooms along the sides. Dazzling cases dotted every wall. So much to see! Gail had one small piece

of jade. Here there was a whole case of jade. There were diamonds and rubies and emeralds, but the most interesting were minerals Gail had never heard of.

"You like it?" Joyce asked.

"It's absolutely the most . . ." Gail couldn't think of a word to describe what she was seeing. *Fantastic* was too weak.

Sometime later, Gail turned away from one case and started toward the next. There stood Joyce, holding her hair back from her face with both hands while she pressed her forehead against the glass.

Gail crept toward her silently. She lowered her head against the case and turned to look up into Joyce's face. Instantly, Joyce straightened and flipped her hair back over her eyes.

"What are you looking at?" Her voice was angry.

"I was trying to see your face, Joyce. Why do you keep it hidden?"

"I'm-ugly-look-at-those-garnets." She said it all as one word so that Gail didn't have a chance to say more about her face.

It took them several hours to see all of the gems and minerals. Returning through the Biology of Man room, Joyce stopped to study several exhibits. Gail looked at one that showed how human babies develop before they are born.

Then they stopped at one of the shops. Gail planned to buy a postcard for her bulletin board, but she found a paperback about rocks that she just had to have. She counted her money carefully. She wouldn't need money for a phone call because she wouldn't get lost. She didn't need much lunch either. She bought the book and had a muffin and a glass of water when they went to the cafeteria.

After lunch, they went to visit their old friends the dinosaurs. The huge Brontosaurus had always been her favorite, but this time she discovered Triceratops, who had a horn on his nose and two other horns.

Vowing to return very soon, she and Joyce went through the basement and into the subway. They made the two subway changes without any problem. The Queens train was crowded, but they both found seats though they were not together. Gail opened her new book and began to read. It was written for adults and had words like *cohesion* and *octahedral*.

She was concentrating so hard that she blocked out the subway and the people around her until she heard her name called. Joyce sounded desperate. Gail looked up. The train had stopped. She jumped to her feet and ran to the door. She caught a glimpse of Joyce on the other side of the door as it closed between them.

"Get off at the next stop and . . ." Joyce's voice faded as the train pulled out of the station.

And what? Gail asked herself. The train gathered speed and was swaying from side to side. Lights of a station appeared ahead but the train didn't slow down. They rushed through the station, and the lights were just streaks through the dirty windows. They sped through another station and another. Was it a runaway train? Was it never going to stop? She looked around at the other passengers. They were either reading or sleeping or staring straight ahead. Not a friend among them.

At that moment, the subway stopped and the lights went out. Gail felt a huge and growing lump in her stomach. There was a little light shining into the car from the tunnel. She looked at the people in the car. The readers had closed their books and papers. "Don't you know we're stuck down here?" Gail wanted to shout. Instead she put the back of her hand into her mouth.

The lump in her stomach was pressing against her lungs. Her breath came in little short gasps. Just then the train jerked, whirred, and started rumbling into a station.

As soon as the door slid open, Gail was out on the platform. She ran to a bench and started emptying her pockets. A notebook, a pencil, three pennies and a nickel. She couldn't make a phone call with three pennies and a nickel. Besides, frightened as she was, Gail didn't want to call her parents. They'd never let her go by herself on the subway again.

Everyone who had gotten off the train with Gail had gone. The platform was empty except for one little old lady with a black shawl over her head.

"Don't talk to strangers," her mother had said. But really, this was a sweet little old lady. Or was she a witch? Gail walked toward her.

"Please madam," she said in her polite voice, "could you tell me how to get back to Roosevelt Avenue?"

The old lady stared up at her. Then she began to shake her head slowly from side to side. "Solly, no Anglish," she whispered.

"I'm sorry too," Gail said. She felt tears rising behind her eyes. "You don't know how sorry."

The old lady reached out and patted her hand.

7

Gail sat down on a bench not far from the old lady. Other people were beginning to fill the platform as Gail took out her map and studied it carefully. She found the Roosevelt Avenue station, near her home. After that came five local stations, the ones they had sped on through. The next express station was Continental Avenue. Gail looked up at a sign that said Continental Avenue. That was reassuring.

Just then a rumble, growing louder and louder, broke the silence. She looked back. There was no train coming. Then she looked across the tracks toward poles. Through the poles she could see another row of tracks and another platform with people standing on it. A train pulled into view on the other side of the poles. That was it! That train was going in the opposite direction of the one Gail had been on. All she had to do was to find the way to that platform and take that train, or one coming from the same direction, back to Roosevelt Avenue.

The lump in Gail's stomach vanished as she ran up a flight of steps to a huge, gray station. The station was filled with clattering roars as the train she had just seen pulled out. That did not worry her. She knew that another train would be coming soon.

Instead of getting quieter, the station became even noisier. She looked down the stairs she had just come up and saw that another train was coming in from Roosevelt Avenue. Gail read the signs in the station and headed toward stairs with a To Manhattan sign above them. She folded her map and put it in her pocket.

"Gail, Gail Walden." Joyce was standing at the top of the stairs that Gail had just come up. Her head was thrown back and she was shouting at the top of her lungs. People in the station had all stopped to stare at this strange child. Gail stared, too. Joyce's hair was back off her face. She had freckles, masses of freckles.

"Here I am," Gail called, and the two girls ran toward one another.

Joyce pulled her hair down over her face as she ran. Gail was not much of a hugger, but she could have hugged Joyce just then. She didn't. She just punched her lightly on the shoulder.

"I'm sure glad to see you," she said.

"Same here. I didn't want to call your folks until I'd looked for you myself. They'd have had fits."

"Boy would they!" Gail giggled. "I've already figured out how to get back."

"Were you scared?" Joyce asked as they stood waiting for the train to take them back to Roosevelt Avenue.

"The lights went out, and I asked a woman for directions and she couldn't speak English. I almost went into a panic." Gail laughed. It seemed like a fun adventure now that Joyce was there to share it with her.

"What are you going to tell your folks?"

"Everything—except about the trip to Continental Avenue. I'll just forget to tell them that. I'm hungry. Come to my house and we'll have something to eat."

This time, when they got to Roosevelt Avenue, they got off the train together. They walked home. Matthew was coming into the building with his bat over his shoulder.

"Hi," Gail said. "Been playing ball?"

"Yah." Matthew walked on toward the stairs. The girls followed him.

"We're coming back from the Museum of Natural History," Gail said casually.

"Who took you?"

"No one. We went by ourselves on the subway."

"I don't believe it." Matthew turned and looked at them.

"Well we did. There's nothing to it if you have two subway tokens and can read a map."

Joyce made a strange gurgling sound, but she did not giggle.

Joyce stayed for dinner. While they were eating, her parents asked lots of questions about their trip.

"When can I go on the subway alone?" Benji asked his parents.

Gail laughed. "A stupid kid like you? You can't even read very well, let alone read a subway map. You'd get lost before you got to Roosevelt Avenue."

"You can go on the subway when you're in the fifth grade," Dad said.

After dinner, Gail and Joyce chose the five rocks Gail would use for her exhibit. They did the streak test on them with a tile Dad had given her. It was amazing. One of the rocks looked solid black, but when they scratched it the tile made a red streak.

They also did the hardness tests. They scratched the rocks with their fingernails first, then with a penny and a knife blade, and finally with a steel file.

"I wish I had a diamond," Gail sighed. "It would make a scratch on all of these rocks."

"I have a diamond you can use," Joyce said.

"Really?"

"It's just a little diamond in a locket that my grandmother gave me for my birthday. I can't take the locket to school, but you can bring your rocks to my house next Saturday and we'll try scratching them with it. We might just as well use the locket for something. I don't wear it." She laughed. A bitter, nonfunny laugh. "My brother says it looks like a ribbon on a pig's tail."

49

Gail was shocked. "What a terrible thing to say. Besides, I saw your face today." Gail spoke slowly and very carefully. "I thought it was a very nice looking face. I was sure glad to see it."

"You'd have been glad to see my face if I were the spitting image of a rhino. You'd have been glad to see anyone you knew." Joyce's laugh was real this time.

The next Saturday, Gail took her science fair rocks to Joyce's apartment. Joyce's tiny room was so crowded there was scarcely room to walk. In addition to a narrow bed and a small dresser, it contained three burbling aquariums and several large jars with fish. Some of the fish were brightly colored. Some had beautiful tails like plumes.

"All from two little gray fish," Joyce said proudly.

"But this one is mostly red and yellow!"

"That's Oscar Number Seven. He's going to the pet store next week. I'm in business, you know. I take my most beautiful guppies to the pet store and trade them for equipment. The owner says I'm his best breeder."

"How can you part with them?"

"How can I not part with them?" Joyce laughed. "Guppies have about a hundred babies at a time, and they have them every couple of months. Besides, I'm not particularly interested in color. I want to breed the largest guppy ever seen with the longest, fullest tail."

Gail examined each fish tank while Joyce ex-

plained how she was planning to produce her super guppy. Then they spread Gail's rocks out on a newspaper, and Joyce went to her dresser to get the locket.

"Hi, Ugly." Joyce's brother was standing in the doorway. He was fifteen, and he had red hair and freckles. "Who's your friend?"

"My name is Gail Walden, and I think it is horrible for you to call Joyce ugly. You have plenty of freckles."

"Right. But my nose doesn't look like a Ping-Pong ball." He walked out of the room.

"He's nasty," Gail said.

"Oldest children are often mean to their younger brothers and sisters."

"Why doesn't your mother stop him?"

"Do your parents stop you from calling Benji stupid?"

"That's different." Gail felt uneasy.

"Why is it different?"

"Well . . ." Gail couldn't think of a thing to say in her own defense. "Maybe I won't call him stupid anymore."

"Fine. Don't."

Gail really did try to stop calling Benji stupid. He was probably just as smart as any other kid his age. She tried to remind herself of that fact. She worked on her be-kind-to-Benji project for three days, Sunday, Monday and Tuesday. Wednesday she quit. He didn't deserve kindness. He didn't deserve anything so much as a slap in the face.

C·H·A·P·T·E·R

"When I came in this evening, I met Morrison in the elevator," Dad said Wednesday night at dinner. "He has tickets to the Columbia-Yale football game Saturday. He invited us to go with him and Matthew."

"Great," shouted Gail.

Dad looked at her in alarm. "I'm sorry, Gail," he said. "He invited Benji and me. He only has four tickets. Want to go, Benji?"

"Boy, do I!" Benji sighed happily. "Columbia-Yale. Boy oh boy!"

Gail pushed her plate away angrily and left the table. She was mad, deep down disgusted mad. At Mr. Morrison for not inviting her. At Matthew, who could have said, "Let's invite Gail." At Benji, her stinking little brother. At her father. He had betrayed her, that's what he had done.

She slammed her bedroom door. She lay down on her bed and thumped her fist into her pillow. She kicked her feet.

Pretty soon there was a knock on her door. "I've brought your dinner, Gail," her mother said softly.

"I don't want it. I'm never going to eat again."

Mother opened the door and put Gail's plate on her desk. Then she sat down beside her on the bed.

"I know you're disappointed, Gail, but Mr. Morrison has obviously planned a men-and-boys outing. You and I will do something special on Saturday. We'll go to the ballet. Lunch first and then the ballet. Won't that be fun?"

"No."

"Please get up and eat your dinner. We'll talk about the ballet again. Try to remember how much Benji will enjoy going to the game with his father." Mother closed the door softly behind her.

Gail considered starving herself, but her plate held fried chicken, which she particularly liked. She ate.

The next day, Matthew was the one chosen to put the math homework answers on the blackboard. Gail glared at him with her eyes and hated him in her heart. Matthew was going to a football game with her stupid baby brother. Why? Because Benji was male. She thought about cutting off her ponytail. If she looked like a boy, could she go to the football game? Should she take up sports? She could practice until she was better than any of the boys. Why should she? She didn't want to be Matthew's friend. She hated Matthew.

All day she thought about how much she hated him. After school, Matthew and his friends were all standing in the school yard in a tight cluster, talking and shouting. Gail walked right up to them and said, "Hi." They didn't even turn around.

"Hey, Matthew," she said in a loud voice. "Remember the time you got your head stuck between the posts on the stairway?"

That got their attention. All the boys turned to look at Gail.

"No kidding?" Peter turned back to Matthew. "Did you really get your head stuck? What happened?"

Before Matthew had a chance to answer, Gail told them that Matthew's mother had called the fire department. "Then just as the firemen were running up the stairs, Matthew wiggled and his head popped out."

The boys laughed and started to walk on.

"That wasn't as funny as the time he gulped down a bottle of soda just before he got on the merry-go-round."

"Then what happened?" asked Jay.

"Stop it, Gail," Matthew hissed.

She ignored him. "He upchucked all over his horse."

The boys all clustered around her, waiting for the next story—except Matthew. He kept grabbing at Jay's sleeve, urging him to walk away. Gail was important. Everyone wanted to hear what she had to say. She smiled smugly, thinking fast. She had to hang on to this moment when Matthew was hurting and she, Gail, was in control.

"By the way," she said in what she hoped was a casual manner. "Did you know that Matthew has a big black birthmark on his bottom?"

The boys all laughed.

"How do you know?" Peter asked.

"We used to take baths together."

Gail turned her back and walked away from the boys. What power! She sauntered down the street, grinning and enjoying the bombshell she had planted. Now she knew why *sweet* was the word used to describe revenge. She had had her revenge, and it was sweet indeed!

Gradually, another feeling began to sneak in among her feelings of triumph. She remembered Matthew's face. At first it had been red. But when she told about the birthmark, it had turned white.

By the time she got home, Gail was feeling miserable. "We used to take baths together," kept ringing in her ears. She went to her room and stayed there until dinnertime. Each time the telephone rang, Gail's stomach leapt to her throat. What if someone told her parents? How could she ever explain what she had done?

That night she couldn't sleep, and the next morning she couldn't eat her breakfast. She planned to skip school, but she couldn't think of anything to do all day. She got to the school yard after her class had gone up. She slipped into her seat, hoping no one had seen her.

"We used to take baths together . . . baths together . . . baths together."

She couldn't hear what the teacher was saying. She couldn't read the words in her book. Finally, she took a sheet of paper out of her notebook. This is what she wrote:

> Dear Matthew,
> I am very, very sorry.
> > Your friend,
> > Gail

When she got up to sharpen her pencil, she dropped the note on his desk. Back in her seat, she watched the back of his head, but he never turned around. Just as they were packing up their books to go home, Matthew dropped a note on her desk. This is what he had written:

> Gail:
> Just leave me alone.
> > Your former friend,
> > Matthew

Gail went home and went to bed. She did not get up for dinner. Her mother took her temperature and said it was normal.

"Do you hurt someplace?" Mother asked.

"All over."

"But I had planned such a nice day for us tomorrow while the men are at their game. I couldn't get tickets for the ballet, but I thought we could have lunch at the Metropolitan Museum and then take in a movie. Just the two of us."

"I'm too sick," moaned Gail.

She was sick. She was sick with fear and shame. Sometimes she hoped that Matthew would tell on her. Then her father could yell at her, and it would all be over.

Dad and Benji left before lunch the next day. When they came home, Gail was lying on the couch in the living room watching TV. Both Benji and her father were smiling. They smelled of cold fresh air. Benji was singing fight songs and telling his mother about the player who had to be carried off the field and the impossible touchdown in the last minute. Gail went back to her room.

Monday Gail's mother took her to the doctor. He jabbed her and thumped her and took blood from her finger and shone lights in her eyes, and said he couldn't find a thing wrong with her.

Tuesday her mother insisted she go to school.

Wednesday the teacher called her out in the hall.

"What is the matter with you, Gail? Do you feel ill? Perhaps you should see a doctor? You haven't been doing your homework. You haven't been contributing to class discussions. You're just not yourself."

"I went to the doctor on Monday. There is nothing wrong with me."

Joyce tried to find out what was the matter with her, too. Joyce's guppies had produced again, the biggest, longest-tailed guppies yet. She wanted to show them to Gail. Gail didn't care about Joyce's guppies. She didn't care about anything.

C·H·A·P·T·E·R

9

Friday Gail walked home beside Amanda. She wasn't with Amanda; she didn't even hear Amanda's chatter during the first block of the walk. After that, Amanda was silent until they entered the lobby of their building, and Amanda began to pat her arm until she had Gail's attention.

"I think I know how you feel," Amanda said softly.

How could Amanda know how she felt? Gail turned away.

"You remind me of the way I acted when my mother died."

Gail stared at her. "But you couldn't help it that your mother died. It wasn't your fault. This was all my . . ." Gail began to cry, and she didn't even try to hide her tears.

Amanda led her to the elevator and up to the sixth floor. When she had unlocked the door to her apartment, she shoved her toward her frilly room.

"Just lie on my bed and cry until you're through crying," Amanda said, throwing back the pink quilted bedspread. "I'll tell your mother you're with me."

When Gail heard the apartment door close and knew she was alone, she cried aloud. Her whole body shook with sobs; her face felt burning hot.

At last the storm was over. Gail sat up and looked around her. On the dressing table was a photograph of a lovely lady, Amanda's mother. Gail could hardly remember her.

There was a knock on the door. "Do you want me to come in?" Amanda asked.

"Yes," answered Gail.

Amanda came and sat on the floor in front of Gail. "You feel better?"

Gail nodded. She knew Amanda expected to hear what it was that was bothering her. Gail couldn't tell Amanda. She knew she would never tell anyone.

"I've been looking at the picture of your mother. She was very beautiful. I think you look a lot like her, Amanda."

"Do you?" Amanda's whole face lit up. "My mother was always so well-groomed. She had such lovely silky hair. I thought she was the prettiest mother at the park."

"You're right. Of all the mothers who sat on benches watching us play when we were little, your mother was the prettiest. I wonder if she knows how neat and well dressed you are. She'd be very proud

of you." Gail got up and straightened her skirt and pushed her hair back in her ponytail. "Thank you, Amanda. You've . . . I . . ." Gail didn't know how to say what she was thinking.

"I'm glad, Gail."

Gail walked down the stairs to her apartment feeling better than she had for a long time. She supposed she would always miss Matthew. He had been a good friend. She knew she would always be sorry she had embarrassed him in front of his new friends. But her body didn't feel stiff and achy anymore, and her eyes didn't burn.

She went to the kitchen where her mother was preparing dinner. She wasn't as pretty as Amanda's mother, but she was a good mother. She hugged her, and her mother hugged her back.

"You know why Amanda is always so well dressed and shiny?" she asked. "It's because she wants to look like her mother. Did you know that?"

Mother kissed her, but she didn't say anything.

"I wish I'd been nicer to her then. I guess I was just too busy having fun with Matthew. That wasn't good. . . ."

"No, but you were very young then, younger than Benji is now. Go wash up for dinner." Mother gave her a hurry-up pat on the bottom.

After dinner, Gail worked on her rock exhibit.

Saturday was a golden fall day, and Dad announced that they were all going to the country to look at the colors of the turning trees.

"Oh boy," shouted Benji. "Can Joey come too?"

"You may invite him," said Dad. "You may invite a friend, too, Gail."

Gail was about to say that she didn't have a friend, and then she thought of Amanda. She ran up to invite Amanda, but no one answered when she rang the bell. She came back to her own apartment and phoned Joyce. Within an hour, she and Joyce and Benji and Joey were packed into the backseat of the car heading out of the city.

They drove a long way. As they went north the colors became more vivid. Even Gail, who usually thought scenery was a bore, found herself gasping with joy.

They had hamburgers and then they drove to a state park, where they got out of the car and hiked. Their footsteps make crunchy sounds on the brittle leaves. Gail found three interesting rocks. Joyce found two, which she gave to Gail for her collection.

On the way home, they stopped at a roadside stand and bought apples and cider. Gail whispered to her mother. When her mother nodded, Gail ran back to where Joyce was studying all the different kinds of squashes and invited her to spend the night. Of course Gail couldn't see her friend's face, but she had a feeling that she was smiling.

Dad dropped the girls off in front of Joyce's apartment house. They gave Joyce's mother a bag of apples and asked if Joyce could spend the night. She could.

They stopped at the library. There sat Matthew hunched at a table with a stack of books in front of him and a scowl on his face. Joyce walked right up to him.

"Hi, Matthew. What's your problem?"

"The science fair." He groaned. "I don't have a project."

Gail went to a low bench near the table where Matthew sat so she could hear what Joyce and Matthew were saying. She couldn't join them, because Matthew was still mad at her. She reached for a book. It was *Curious George*, of all things, Benji's favorite book when he was about four. She opened the book and began turning the pages.

"I thought you and Jay were going to build a catapult," she heard Joyce say. "I think that's a great project."

"Jay's working with Peter on a crystal radio. It's too late to get the materials and build a catapult by myself."

So Matthew's friend had let him down! Gail could feel herself grinning, and then she was ashamed of herself for being glad. She heard a chair scrape and knew that Joyce was sitting down beside Matthew.

"Maybe I can help," Joyce suggested. "Amanda's going to do a solar system, so you won't want to do that. There isn't time to train a gerbil to run a maze. Or to grow anything. Maybe something about gravity. Hey, Gail, come help us find a project for Matthew."

Gail jumped up and headed for the table.

"I don't want your help," Matthew shouted, grabbing a book from Joyce. He pushed past Gail and headed for the check-out desk.

Gail slid down into the chair Matthew had left. Joyce shook her head, bewildered.

"I wonder why he doesn't want my help," Joyce said.

"Because he's mad at *me*."

"You and Matthew have been best friends for as long as I can remember."

"He hasn't talked to me since school started. We were going to do the rock project together. He told me to collect rocks, and I did. I collected rocks all summer. He didn't bring one home. He's one nasty kid." Gail stared down at her hands on the table in front of her. "I'm a nasty kid, too," she whispered. "I did something really mean to Matthew."

"Did you apologize?"

"Yes. I wrote him a note telling him I was sorry. He wrote back and told me to leave him alone. We had fights when we were little, but they didn't last. Why doesn't he want to be my friend now?"

"He's like my brother. In fifth grade, my brother belonged to a club called the Girl Haters."

"What did they do in their club?"

"They played ball and made up rules. One rule was that no member could talk to a girl except during class, and then only if it were necessary."

"Does your brother still belong to that club?"

"No way! He and his friends talk about girls all the time. It's disgusting! Which girl has the prettiest

hair. Which girl has the sweetest voice. Yuk! After school, he calls up a girl named Suzie and they talk for hours. He loves girls now, except for me. He still hates me." Joyce laughed as if she didn't care that her brother hated her. "Matthew will like girls someday, I'll bet."

"He won't like me."

"Maybe he will and maybe he won't. There's nothing you can do about it now, so just forget it. Too bad he wouldn't let us help with his project, but that's his problem."

After dinner, Gail and Joyce watched an old movie on TV while they ate popcorn and drank cider. From time to time, Gail thought about Matthew and his science fair project.

She thought about it again after they were in bed, and in the morning when she woke up. Then she opened her eyes and watched Joyce. Joyce obviously thought Gail was still sleeping.

Joyce had brushed all of her hair back off her face. There was no birthmark. Joyce's nose was not enormous; it was fat and squat. She had freckles, lots and lots of them, like her brother. Her face wasn't beautiful, but it was friendly and nice. Joyce made two parts in her lovely hair. She brushed the side sections forward over her cheeks and the top section straight down over her nose.

Gail got out of bed silently and went to her dresser and picked up a tiny barrette. "Why don't you just pull that center section a little bit to one side?" she whispered.

"I'd feel so strange."

"Try it. You can always put it back if you don't like it that way."

Joyce went to the mirror and carefully pulled the center section of her hair a little to the side and held it with the barrette.

"I like it," said Gail. "Do you?"

"I can see better," said Joyce.

"How nice you look, Joyce," Mother said when the girls went to the kitchen for breakfast.

Joyce smiled, and Gail could see a little part of her smile.

C · H · A · P · T · E · R

10

Joyce left soon after breakfast and Gail went to her room to think, hard and for a long time. She read the book she had bought at the Museum of Natural History. She examined the rocks on her shelves and finally selected eight of them. She put the rocks and the book in a paper bag and sat down at her desk to write a letter. She wrote a long letter—and tore it up. And another. At last she shrugged her shoulders and wrote this:

> Matthew,
> Collecting rocks was your idea. Here are
> some and a book. See page 92. Please return
> the book and the Indian arrowhead when
> the science fair is over.
> > Gail

She stapled the note to the bag and took it upstairs and put it in front of Matthew's door. Then she rang the bell, not her usual three short rings but one long one. She ran back to the stairway and down to her own apartment.

Gail's exhibit was in two parts. A box held all of the equipment she had used, except the diamond, and the five rocks she had tested. A poster explained about the tests, the results of each test, and Gail's decisions about the identity of the five rocks. Her father helped her carry it to school on Wednesday. Benji walked with them, proudly carrying his burglar alarm.

Everyone in Gail's class was early that morning. Long before the first bell, each one had put an exhibit on a desk and was busy protecting it from bumps. At the same time, each one was trying to see everyone else's project.

As soon as the bell rang, Mrs. Johnson announced that each person would bring his or her project to the front of the room and explain it to the rest of the class. Amanda had made a model of the solar system using different sized balls to represent each planet and a big yellow balloon for the sun. The crystal radio Jay and Peter had made really worked.

Joyce's exhibit wouldn't fit on her desk so she had placed it on the table in the library corner, behind a rolling blackboard. When she pushed the blackboard aside and turned to face the class to explain her experiment, each child seemed to catch his breath. Gail wondered which surprised them most, Joyce's face or Joyce's project. She still had her side hair brushed over her cheeks but the top section was pulled to one side with a barrette larger than the one Gail had given her. Her blue eyes sparkled as she talked about her guppies.

The two original guppies were in one jar. Another jar was labeled The Midpoint of the Experiment. The third jar contained large guppies with huge sweeping tails. It was labeled Joyce's Giant Guppies. Behind the jars was a chart that showed how she had bred the largest guppies with the best tails from each brood. Another chart was titled Principles of Genetics. When Joyce returned to her seat, everyone in the room began to clap.

Gail's exhibit wasn't as spectacular as Joyce's, but she showed it with pride. No one clapped when she returned to her seat, but something better happened.

"I think Gail's exhibit is very scientific," announced Matthew.

"It certainly is," said Mrs. Johnson. "I see you have a rock project, too. Will you show it to us now?"

Gail was not surprised at Matthew's exhibit—it was the one she had suggested. She was surprised at how well he had done it. He'd had so little time. He explained that some rocks are formed by nature, like the rocks smoothed by the sea. He said that others were formed by men and that you could look at them and tell what kinds of tools were used. He showed a rock cut with a saw and the arrowhead shaped by primitive tools.

Mrs. Johnson suggested that he place his exhibit beside Gail's when they set them up in the gym. "Your projects complement one another."

When everyone had shown his work, they took their projects to the table reserved for their class in the gym. Gail and Matthew worked in silence. Then Gail turned to look for Joyce. She was surrounded by children trying to get close looks at the guppies. Gail started toward her when she felt a familiar punch on her shoulder.

"Thanks, old pal," Matthew whispered.

She turned, and he grinned at her.

"Hey Matthew," Jay called as he walked toward them. "How come you and Gail both have rock exhibits? I thought you were through being friends with her. You said you hated girls."

"It just happened," Gail said. She smiled at Matthew.

And Matthew grinned at her again before he walked away with Jay.

Thursday Gail's class visited the gym to see what other classes had done. Gail made a special effort to find Benji's burglar alarm. It was, she decided, very impressive compared with the other exhibits from his class, most of which involved beans.

Thursday night the parents came to see the science exhibits.

Friday the winners were announced. To no one's surprise, Joyce was declared the school winner. Her

guppies would be included in the city-wide science fair. The surprise was that on that day Joyce wore a band that held all of her hair back off her face.

Saturday was a rainy, windy, sleety day. Gail was thinking about maybe starting to clean her room when she heard three short taps on the doorbell. She ran to admit Matthew.

He handed her her rocks and book. "Thanks." He stood staring down at his sneakers while Gail waited to hear what else he had to say. "Ever play Diplomacy?" he asked.

Gail shook her head.

"It's Jay's game. He's coming over with it, but we need more than two. You and Amanda? Mom says we can send out for pizza and play all day."

Gail wondered why they couldn't play Monopoly, and she was about to ask when Matthew continued. "It's a better game than Monopoly. Whole countries, not just houses and hotels. You'll like it."

"Sure." Gail grinned at him. "But first I have to clean my room."

"So hurry up. I know how fast you can clean it when you want to." He gave her a little punch on the shoulder before he ran up to Amanda's.

Gail stripped the sheets from her bed and hauled the dirty clothes out from under it. She wondered about this new game. Could five play it, or six? They could invite Joyce and maybe Peter. She'd see when she got to Matthew's.

ABOUT THE AUTHOR

LOUANN GAEDDERT is the author of *The Kid With the Red Suspenders, Just Like Sisters,* and other books. She says, "I have set this, my tenth book for young people, in the New York neighborhood where I live. The school is similar to the one my children attended. My daughter was a rock hound like Gail, and my son was a sports enthusiast like Matthew. Otherwise the story is entirely fictitious."

The Gaedderts live in the borough of Queens, in New York City.

ABOUT THE ILLUSTRATOR

MARY BETH SCHWARK, who illustrated *The Kid With the Red Suspenders,* is a commercial graphic artist as well as an illustrator. She lives in Ortonville, Michigan.